Twisted Intimacies

Volume 2

An Anthology of 17 Highly Erotic Short Stories

Saicka Ross

TWISTED INTIMACIES

First edition. June 27, 2024.

Copyright © 2024 Saicka Ross.

ISBN: 979-8227653536

Written by Saicka Ross.

Also by Saicka Ross

Twisted Intimacies
Twisted Intimacies
Twisted Intimacies

Embark on a sultry odyssey of carnal delight with "Twisted Intimacies Volume 2: An Anthology of 17 Highly Erotic Short Stories." Delve deeper into the realms of human desire as you savor each titillating tale in this exquisite second edition. Prepare to lose yourself in intricate narratives brimming with raw emotion, surprising twists, and scintillating encounters.

Discover the power of personal growth through erotic experiences in these carefully curated vignettes, handpicked from a wealth of submissions received since the release of Volume 1. Explore fresh perspectives, taboo subjects, and innovative approaches to sexual expression as you navigate this delectable assortment of stories designed to stimulate both mind and body.

Diversify your literary palette by immersing yourself in a rich array of character backgrounds, evocative locales, and complex dynamics. Each selection presents a unique blend of passion, curiosity, and tension, inviting readers to push past comfort zones and venture boldly into uncharted territories.

Whether you're drawn to whispered secrets shared between strangers, stolen moments of illicit pleasure, or the satisfaction found in satisfying long-held fantasies, "Twisted Intimacies Volume 2" promises a veritable feast of temptations tailor-made for adventurous souls. Allow yourself to become entranced by the artistry woven throughout these pages, skillfully crafted by seasoned writers eager to seduce even the most discerning connoisseurs of erotica.

Indulge in this sumptuous banquet of explicit scenes, vivid imagery, and thoughtful reflections on what it means to seek – and find – fulfillment in a world teeming with possibilities. With so much variety packed into one tantalizing package, there's never been a better time to give in to your baser instincts and indulge in the pleasures that await within the pages of "Twisted Intimacies Volume 2." Don't miss out – satisfy your cravings now!

Plan with Karim

I will speak in the 1st person and put the real or false names, it doesn't matter.

My name is Olivier, I am 40 years old, and I am very submissive. I like domination and giving myself to other guys, you will quickly understand that.

I'm coming to tell you my stories because I've been a big fan of yours for years and I said to myself that it was my turn to do my part.

The other day, I was hanging out on grindr, the pumpers, and the rebeus, and one of my regulars, whose name is Karim 50 years old 20x6, so rather appetizing, contacted me on a Sunday afternoon and I really liked his approach , I quote: "You come, I fuck you, and you offer me your bitch ass, and you leave". Simple, clean and precise as they say. I replied: "ok, I'll be there for 30-35" and then to close he said: "Be quick before I change my mind."

Then I arrived at his house and.....

So I arrive at his house, he is very cordial, this is a game between consenting adults, so apart from no submission and humiliation (I want to make this clear because all my plans are based on this relationship of trust).

On the other hand, I get into the game very quickly and get naked and usually he tells me to lay on the bed and then he tells me to lean on the kitchen counter, ass stretched, good arched, legs spread, puts gel on me, and slowly penetrates me with his big, big cock, I remember that it is 20 cm long, 6 cm wide and hard as concrete.

At this point, I start moaning continuously and try to push my hole as much as possible in order to widen the passage. I sniff poppers too.

Then the comings and goings begin and there it is the height of pleasure that invades me. I start squealing continuously and panting like a dog.

Then he decides to change and try something else, he asks me to sit on a counter seat with my ass back on the seat and stay like that. I comply. I remind you that I love obeying orders and being a good slut.

At this precise moment he penetrates me with a sharp blow all the way to the bottom, I immediately flattened myself on the counter and I didn't even cry out because my breathing was cut off with surprise and pleasure, I I had never been penetrated so deeply in this way and there he began his thrusts. I squealed, I squealed, without stopping and he said salacious words to me which excited me even more.

The situation no longer suited him, he ordered me to go and get on all fours on the bed where he shoved his organ in one go and made me scream with happiness as he shook my prostate and felt all his virility inside me. 'man. My presumed role was now completely assumed,I was the dog, he was the master, and that suited me and I took great pleasure in it.

He put me on the side and pounded me with all his strength, I was panting more and more jerkily and out of breath because his thrusts almost made me hit my head against the wall and he insulted me as a female dog. I could only approve as I enjoyed it so much and wanted to never stop this magical moment.

He ended up telling me that he was going to cum, and at that precise moment, he accelerated the thrusts and I began to scream with the satisfaction I was feeling as the sexual tension was at its peak.

Finally, I asked him to empty the condom, full to the brim, over my buttocks.

As agreed, I got dressed in my light gray shorts and left his house. My role was over and I left, getting in my car and stopping for a quick run down the road to my house.

When I got home I saw myself in the mirror, my bottom was soaked and it was hard not to understand what it was because it was so visible through the fabric that I had gotten my behind soiled.

What were people thinking during the races? Some of the looks were weird... I understood better why and felt ashamed and excited at the same time as perhaps a daddy said to himself in his corner "but what a female dog that is" and discreetly jerked off on me once he got home.

There you go, this true story with Karim has come to an end, I have many others with him as well as others that I will be happy to tell you another time.

Big kisses to all.

Olivier.

PS: I love the way he summons me to his house where I arrive at the speed of light, always with salacious words while outside of the plan he knows how to respect me and everything is just staged in the end. However, during the scenarios I love to play along like a little (big?) slut. I dream of doing the same kind of plan but with 2-3 more guys who take me wildly and with whom I scream with pleasure.

For the moment he doesn't want to fuck me without a condom but I hope one day to receive everything in my foundation (I'm on prep). Plus he squirts a phenomenal amount of juice, I had the experience hmmmm. It is planned that we will do a shot where we film in order to broadcast it without anyone seeing my face.. I am looking forward to this very naughty shot!

A boss and an employee

Today I have to meet a young woman aged 24. According to her file she is a serious young woman, who knows what she wants. She is dark, tall, thin and has a large chest. I feel that I'm going to have fun with her, she'll be my new little submissive.

Three knocks are heard on my door, I then let out a "Come in!" » and I finally see this young woman, very beautiful indeed. I smiled softly and asked her to sit in front of me, she was wearing a little black dress that hugged her body perfectly, as shoes they were white pumps that also matched her white blazer. I look at her for a long time, then I ask her a few questions.

"Why do you want to do this job?

-Without boasting ma'am, I think I'm perfect for this position.

-Really ? And what are you ready to do?

-Everything, really everything. »

I then smirked, proud of what she had just said, she was in deep trouble, she doesn't know what she's gotten herself into.

"Perfect, you're hired, my dear. Now come to me and take off your clothes.

-Wh..What?

-You understood me very well, my darling, come on.

-But I'm supposed to work!

-Yes you will do it later, now take off your clothes before I get angry!

»

I could see in her eyes that she was afraid, she didn't understand what happened to her and so much the better, all of this excites me enormously, I get up before facing her, she doesn't move a foot , I then frown and take off her blazer looking into her pretty blue eyes, then I slowly undo her zipper.

"- Poor thing, you are going to be punished, do you know that?

-But I didn't do anything.

-I gave you an order, you didn't do it, little bitch.

-Excuse me.

-It's too late. »

So I throw her dress to the floor and unhook her black lace bra, I look at her pretty generous chest and whip one of her breasts with the tips of my fingers, she then lets out little cries of pain which makes me 'excited even more, I take one of her nipples before pinching it firmly between my thumb and my index finger, I have fun with rolling it between my fingers, pinching it strongly and pulling it, she was in pain, I knew it but I didn't care, she was punished.

After a few minutes of seeing her suffer I stop looking into her eyes, I caress her cheek tenderly and smile.

"- Don't make that face my darling, you are magnificent when you are in pain. »

She didn't know what to say, I gave my lips a quick lick before taking off my shirt and my skirt, I smirked while I saw fear in her eyes, I sat down on my desk spreading my legs leaving him a magnificent view of my penis soaked from excitement.

"- Approaches. » I said to her before running a hand through my brown hair, I see her approach with doubtful steps, I still smiled and once she was facing me, I order her to get on her knees and she did.

"Now you're going to lick me."

-Wh..What..?

-You understood me very well, come on.

-No

sorry ?

-I... Yes... Excuse me.

-Well, I have to train you like a little dog. »

Without wasting time, I take her hair firmly and press her face against my privacy, I order her to lick me and so she begins to do it, I smile and close my eyes letting the pleasure take over.

Her tongue slowly caresses my clitoris which makes me feel really good, I let out a few sighs of pleasure while watching her do it.

"That's good, lick my pussy you little slut." Mh, you love him hun, say you love him.

-I love him, yes.

- What do you like ?

-Your pussy ma'am, I love your pussy. »

I smile and force his head back against my wet sex.

After a long minute, I moan softly having reached orgasm, I lift her head strongly and smile seeing her mouth surround my wet, I lift her up and go look for ropes. Once these are in hand, I lay her down on my desk and tie her up, spreading her legs revealing her part covered by her lace panties.

"Your punishment is not over. "

Breton Slut

I am 45 years old, married, and have two children, but this story takes place in August 1994, I was 26 at the time, I had broken up with my girlfriend a few months earlier and I found myself alone for the holidays without knowing where to go. A friend, whose parents had a shack on a Breton island opposite Lorient, asked me to come with him, telling me that there were some girls there who were not very shy.

Arriving at my destination, he took me around the island, showing me the nice spots, introducing me to friends of his... In short, a few days later I met Estelle, a native and pure Breton strain: in her late twenties, a little plump brunette with a nice pair of tits, she was round all over but she was very cute. We hit it off and I told myself that I would make it all the best for four hours!

A few days later I was at the beach and I saw Estelle arriving alone with a two-piece swimsuit slightly too small for her and from which her enormous breasts were well overflowing. She leaned over to give me a kiss and I couldn't help but stare at her tits which were just asking to come out of the swimsuit!

After five minutes of chatting and sunbathing, she suggested that we go for a walk in a small cave that is flooded at high tide but accessible at low tide. The tide being outgoing, we had to swim a little, we even did a little bit of apnea.

So here we are in this cave just lit by the light filtered by the water.

I said to him:

"It's a nice place but it's a little chilly!" »

"Yes, you surprise me, I'm a little cold, don't you want to warm me up? »

"Well with pleasure!"

And there she clings to me... I hold her in my arms, I feel her huge tits crushing on me, the effect is immediate, I start to get hard, she presses herself against me and she looks at me with a small smile.

"Ha! I feel something there "

Sorry but those are your big tits...I can't resist."

She smiles at me and gives me a smack, I kiss her full on the mouth, my hands go down to her buttocks which I knead, I hold her close to me and get more and more hard. I touch her everywhere, my hands go up, I pull on her bikini top, her two enormous breasts appear, they are heavy, soft, I feel them, play with her nipples, suck them, kiss them, knead them and she moans, sigh.

My other hand slips between her thighs, I feel her swimsuit soaked but it's hot, my fingers seep under the fabric: it's smooth, not a hair... I almost tear off her stockings, she's naked in front of me, I get hard, she doesn't say anything, lets herself be done, I get terribly hard but I want her luscious lips, I can't take it anymore:

"Go ahead and suck me..."

She doesn't say anything, squats down, pulls down my swim shorts and does so. Her mouth is hot, she sucks me gently while jerking me off, I lean over to feel her huge heavy breasts, she speeds up, swallows my cock and in my head I say to myself: "What a fucking slut! She likes it!"

I want to eat her pussy and I tell her "come in 69"

I get on my back, the sand is cold, she straddles me, offers me a superb view of her smooth and fleshy pussy, slightly open . I part her lips and plunge my tongue in, it's a mixture of wet and sea water: it's salty. I eat her cunt, her clit, I finger her roughly, she pumps my cock like a whore who wants to make you spit, I suck her clit, nibble her lips, search her cunt, I lick her little hole, I feel her tense, the tongue penetrates gently and she moans. I risk a finger, it goes in easily!

The little slut is already fucked, my index finger in her ass and my thumb in her pussy I eat her clit while fingering her. She wiggles while swallowing my cock which is ready to explode, I risk two fingers in her pussy and two in her ass, she tightens her mouth on my cock, I can't hold back and I spit all my cum which fills her mouth... but she continues to suck me...

My fingers search her, she stands up, she swallows everything, the slut! I finger her roughly, she cums with a long moan while sighing to me "sooooooooooooooo..."

I get hard again, I push her to put her on all fours and take her doggy style.

Then we hear voices, children's laughter, we barely have time to hide and put our jerseys back on. The kids see us and have a start of astonishment:

"Well, what are you doing here?

We answer them in one voice: "like you, we explore!"

The oldest, who must have been 14 years old, looked at us with a little smirk as we left the cave, I'm sure he knew exactly what we had done!

We re-fucked several times in other places but that's other stories, soon you'll know!!

In public toilets

It was last summer but I remember it like it was yesterday... I met a guy on chat and this time I agreed to meet him. I was 19 and he was 24. We arranged to meet at a party that a friend was organizing so as not to end up alone with him. I was dressed in a mini skirt, little white top and red thong bra.

Around 4:30 a.m. everyone started to leave but I wasn't tired. I drank a lot of alcohol that evening and that's probably why I agreed to let John, the chat guy, come with me. We had gotten along well all evening and I felt confident... He suggested that I go for a walk in the public garden... I accepted. We climbed the gate (obviously he took the opportunity to check out my thong, or rather my butt...) then we started walking around...

We acted crazy for about an hour running everywhere... He ran after me and then he grabbed me, squeezed me, stood behind me and touched my butt... I found him really nice... He managed to excite me... I found him quite cute.

Continuing our way we passed public toilets, empty and clean since we had passed the cleaning team. John stops and says to me: "um, it must be pretty good there..." with a smirk. For fun, I responded to his smile, so he said to me: "Come on, let's just take a look... nothing more..." I knew very well what he wanted to do but I knew that If he insists too much I will make it clear to him that I do not do this in public toilets.

Anyway, I am, we go into the WC. He stops in front of the row of cabins and hugs me then kisses me in the face, then on the mouth, then with the tongue, he smelled of beer, it was intoxicating... He began to caress my buttocks then his hand slipped under my skirt reaching the top of the back of my thigh. "He certainly doesn't dare to go any higher" I thought, but I was wrong, he hugged me tighter, pushed me into a cabin, closed the lock before I had time to react. He pinned me against the door, I began to struggle but he said to me: "You have what you want, chick, let yourself do it now!", I replied: "No, not here! Not now, let's see! We're not don't know, you're drunk!"

During the short moment when I was responding to him, he slipped his hand under my skirt, on my buttocks, touched the string of my thong, then his hand, still on my skirt, slid over my left hip to finally arrive at the thong which covered My gender. He kissed me with tenderness and slipped his hand violently under my thong in order to reach the lips of my thong with two fingers. I got wet. It excited him so he left my skirt alone and moved on to my top. He kissed me again, and as his tongue brushed mine, his hand slipped under my top.

Once the kiss was over, he looked me in the eyes, passing his hands around me to unfasten my bra. I still wore my top but my bra didn't cover me. He lifted my top, squared my chest, and said to me: "humm, your nipples are standing, I seem to have an effect on you..." I didn't answer, I only gave him a look allowing him to read the bottom of my thoughts. He rolled my nipples between his fingers and licked them excitedly. I still found it pleasant...

Then he sat me down on the toilet, knelt in front of me, still leaving my chest uncovered. He gently parted my thighs, passed his hands under my skirt, slipped his fingers under my thong, tilted me backwards, pulled my thong to the side, brought his mouth to my sex, then licked me, pushed his tongue as deep as possible. from my vagina. I liked it, he guessed.

He stood up, straightened me too, who was so passive, squared my chest, took out his penis, I felt it, against mine, it was tight and hard... John was hard, all of a sudden I felt my sex watered with a cho and sticky liquid, he had just ejaculated... He shifted my thong to the side and pushed his penis deep into my vagina, then he made little thrusts, just to excite me.

Besides, it worked well, all I wanted to do was shout at him, "Fuck it! Go ahead! Fuck my pussy! You fuck like god!" but no words were willing to come out of my mouth.

Suddenly, he thrust his penis with force and violence deep into mine. I can't help but moan "hummmmmmmmmmmm". He gently took his penis out of mine and closed his fly. Straightened me up, stroked my chest one last time. Stared at me for about 30 seconds in silence. Then suddenly opened the door and ran out.

I stayed there, top pulled up, my bra ungraffitied, mini skirt, legs spread, sitting on a public toilet, in the early morning... I had just had my first sexual experience knelt in front of me, still leaving my chest uncovered.

1st experience

The summer I turned 18, my parents agreed that I go to the seaside with my cousin Jérémy, the same age as me, and one of his childhood friends, Kévin, whom I didn't know.

Arriving at the campsite, we had a secluded spot where we set up our igloo tent, then quickly changed into our swimwear.

I'm athletic, 1.95m tall. well-designed bodybuilding through diligent swimming. My cousin, although smaller than me, is also well built. Kevin was 1.65 m tall, not very muscular, a very thin and very youthful face, very white skin without any hair despite his 19 years.

I was in mini swimming trunks, I love them tight, white to highlight my tan, my cock and my balls.

Jérôme, my cousin, had a pair of red boxers that also fitted his cock and balls well. Kévin wore an infamous pair of faded and distended swim trunks. He seemed shy but very nice.

At the evening meal, I was seated at the table opposite my cousin, Kévin next to him. The 3 of us were talking when I felt a foot caressing the front of my swimming trunks, I laughingly told my cousin to stop his bullshit. He didn't say anything to me and the foot was still caressing my bump. I grabbed the foot, pulling on it and telling my cousin "stop, I'm not a faggot" when I saw

Kevin collapse, I then understood who the foot belonged to. He turned crimson red, told me he wasn't who I thought and that he just wanted to have fun. As he fell, his swimsuit caught on the table and tore, Kévin was lying naked on the floor on his back, I was disturbed to see his big smooth cock on 2 beautiful smooth balls on such a grungy body.

Laughing, I jumped on him and held him firmly on the ground with me lying on top of him, he smiled at me and I felt his cock harden on my stomach, I called him a dirty little faggot and he replied with a disarming smile "so what, does it bother you? », I gave him a big skate to see his reaction, he seemed to like it. I felt my cock harden in my underwear ready to make him crack, I was starting to get a taste for it. I rubbed my stomach on his cock, it was quickly full of Kevin's wetness.

Wanting to upset him, I told him in a nasty tone, well if you dare come suck my cock, and I lay on my back. To my great surprise, Kevin leaned over my mini underwear and began to lick them, then took them down to me and began to lick my balls and my cock. I then felt a great thrill and extreme excitement which made me quickly cum in his mouth, Kevin swallowed all my cum with relish.

Jérémy was watching us all the time, groping himself through his boxers. Excited by this situation, I placed my hand on his bump, he quickly lowered his boxers and for the first time I touched a cock other than mine. She was very stiff, circumcised without any hair, which surprised me. I don't yet know why, I had a crazy desire to suck her. I placed a furtive kiss on the glans, he smelled quite strongly of the male and that excited me even more. Jérémy wiggled and fucked my mouth well, after 5 minutes, he was squirting big jets of sperm into my mouth. Immediately, I appreciated this acrid and salty taste and swallowed it all.

Following this episode, Jérémy revealed to me that he was queer and that Kévin was his boyfriend. I then admitted to him that I had sex with girls but that it left me unsatisfied and that I loved what came to occur. He then suggested that I continue my introduction to fucking between guys. He offered me his ass so I could see if I liked fucking a guy. He lay down on his back on the table, legs raised, his ass offered, my stiff cock passed between his buttocks and with a little thrust my glans perforated his ass, I then began long thrusts in and out in a state second when I felt Kevin caress my buttocks then lick my ass, which excited me even more.

Then Kevin got up and slipped his cock between my buttocks. I was so excited by the situation, I let myself do it when I felt a violent pain as he deflowered my ass. He stayed for a moment without moving while I came back to my senses, then he started thrusting in and out at the same pace as my thrusts in Jeremy's ass. After a long time, I felt an extreme pleasure, like I had never felt, invade me. I ejaculated large jets of sperm in Jeremy's ass, Kevin emptied himself in my ass and Jeremy in my hand . I was exhausted but happy.

The whole vacation was just threesomes in all positions, sucking us, fucking each other in the ass.

We've been a threesome for three years now, still excited to get together to fuck together.

Well managed shared accommodation

I started working very early (almost 19 years old) in Paris. Accommodation is so expensive that I shared a flat with 2 young people a little older than me (21 and 22). I was already of a fairly docile temperament because I was always corrected with the flogger in my childhood and even my adolescence.

Marc, who was 21 years old, took a lot of initiative and was quite direct when he gave instructions on the common areas of the apartment, which suited me very well. Little by little, he would come to my room and also give me orders on how to put my things away. So I was quite admiring of this young man. He noticed and we started having sex.

Obviously, he was the active one and I was the passive one. Everything was going well and quite discreetly until the day he came into my room where nothing was tidy, the dirty socks were lying on the floor and I was waiting for him naked, hoping to get fucked when he arrived. I was naked as a worm on the bed already erect thinking about what I wanted to happen to me. He, standing in front of the door that he had closed, is stunned by the scene, a scene of disorder. He gives me soap and at the same time takes off his belt, which excites me despite the garland.

This situation upset him and he ordered me to lie down on my stomach while turning around in bed. I didn't have to wait long to enjoy the dozen strokes of the belt that I took on my thighs and my little ass. "you understand, I don't want it to start again." he told me. I felt my buttocks hot and reddened by the rust I had just taken and I nodded without response, convinced that he was right and that I was lucky that he was guiding me. He then approached me and caressed my buttocks, I spread them but the desire to give him a blowjob after my correction had never been so strong.

When his caresses led him to finger me, I no longer hesitated, I undid his pants, caressed his boxers then I passed my hand into his boxers to take out his already stretched cock. I got closer and started sucking him with a passion and conviction that I had never had. I licked this cock which was that of the male who had just given me a well-deserved beating, his hardness symbolized for me all his authority. I could only show my docility better than by licking his balls, his beautiful hard cock and without a doubt I longed for him to squirt in my mouth to swallow everything without wasting anything because a man capable of correcting me like that deserved well. He caressed my buttocks and I sucked his beautiful rod until he let go and without effort, I didn't let go and I swallowed well, showing him my full mouth and licking my lips for him to show that I won't waste anything.

"I think you understand well" he said to me and added "it will be better with a flogger or a crop than with my belt". He therefore orders me to go buy the flogger and the riding crop either in a pet store or in a sex shop. The shame of going to buy a flogger in a sex shop therefore leads me to make this purchase in a pet store. I was very humiliated when I went to the checkout because I had the impression that the cashier knew it was for me. It fell on my birthday.

That evening, we had a meal for three and at the end of the meal, I received a gift package. I am very touched and when I unpack it in front of my 2 roommates, I am surprised and ashamed compared to Charles to find a leash and a collar which leave no doubt about their future use. Charles does not seem very surprised and Marc immediately reassures me by declaring that he is also obliged to take care of the education of Charles who agrees with a nod.

"Come on, furry guys, we're going to try our new toys," said Marc. Charles and I get naked, Charles goes to get his collar and leash from his room, Marc takes us on a leash and takes us out onto the balcony on all fours to take us for a walk. Marc then takes the flogger that I bought, asks Marc to stand straight against the wall, hands resting on the wall and me also straight not very far away. Marc starts to slam the flogger on Charles' ass and asks me to jerk off while he does so. I quickly got a hard-on seeing that little ass blushing at Marc's regular actions but I was already thinking that it wouldn't be long before I replaced Charles with his hands against the wall.

Marc got naked too and seeing him hard during the correction turned me on like crazy. The fifteen strokes administered to my roommate's ass ended and I was invited to take the same position. Charles begins to jerk off to the sound of the flogger slapping my buttocks. Oddly enough, the situation makes me hard too.

Marc says that the swift looks good and tells us to stand side by side. The situation is more difficult because I never know which of the two (Charles or me) will be the recipient of the swift blow.

Our buttocks are very red when Marc stops, pointing out that it is exhausting for him to correct us. We let Marc rest and tidy our rooms, the common areas and prepare the meal. Charles and I act together in a very coordinated way. We clearly understood that we must obey, be very respectful among ourselves.

We spent 2 years in shared accommodation under Marc's authority and with the greatest pleasure. Obviously Marc fucked us both, sometimes together in fact, he made fun of us by making us play dykes but we were not allowed to have relations with each other without his authorization.

I had a great time with an authoritarian friend who fucked us copiously and very respectfully. Our corrections were always fair and without violence only with the flogger or the crop on our little asses.

I always appreciate these qualities in a man.

Living with 2 men

Max and I have been living together since we finished our studies about ten years ago. We have a small apartment in Paris. Nobody outside knows that we are homosexual. Between us, Max is the dominant one.

Our sexual relations allow us to give each other good blowjobs and good handjobs but Max sodomizes me and I don't. Little by little, we have organized ourselves and it is me who does the household chores. I take care of the cleaning, the cooking, the shopping, the ironing. It is he who drives the car when we go out and who pays for the restaurant on occasion.

He regularly asks me to feminize myself more and more. I am no longer allowed to pee standing up, I have to sit on the toilet bowls; it is more boring in nature, I have to pull down my pants and squat like the females. I now wear erotic women's underwear, pink thong, jock strap, panties that come off with a knot on the side or a zipper snap underneath. This is how we find our balance. Max has a job as a manager and is often stressed.

In these situations, when he comes home, he asks me to relieve him. I then have to ask him "with my hand, with my mouth or with my little ass?" you understand what I have to do according to his answer. When it is with the hand, I have to masturbate him until his thick and creamy juice comes out only with the hand. It is sometimes difficult to see this beautiful male organ in front of me so close to my face without being able to lick it. I then have to wipe his juice with a paper towel and then I prepare a bath for him.

When the bathtub is full and the foam is abundant, he gets in the bathtub and there, I wash him from his shoulders to his big feet (he wears size 45 shoes) passing by his beautiful male organ that I take care to uncover and caress, then I pass the soap in his beautiful crack of the ass and in his beautiful muscular ass. He sometimes thanks me by licking my cock, I love that. When his request is with my mouth, I have to suck and swallow his seed without wasting the slightest drop.

This would make him angry, the only time I let a few drops of his juice fall on the floor, he made me lick it on the floor. It doesn't hurt me to swallow his cum, he has been used to me for a long time and I like it because I see that he appreciates it. When Max answers me with my little ass, I quickly go get some lubricant and coat my little ass as well as his cock.

Indeed, he has a tail of a good caliber 19 cm long and 5 cm in diameter. I get on all fours, I pass my hand between my legs to guide his member to the entrance of my little hole and there, he takes me by the hips and destroys my ass for a while. From his moan, I understand that he has cum deep inside me. I then allow myself to jerk off to cum too.

But, Max doesn't just empty his balls into my body, he often makes love to me and we fully enjoy it together. He loves making love to me in unusual places. I'm going to tell you some of these romantic adventures with Max.

He likes to park the car in the woods. He sits in the front passenger seat, we caress each other for a long time. I undo his fly, take his beautiful member out of his underwear and approach him to give him a good blowjob. I first take the glans in my mouth, suck it well then salivate all around it. Then, I go down with my tongue along his 19 cm to take his big balls in my mouth one after the other. I love it because I find it's a moment when I feel like I have a handsome male of my own and for me.

Meanwhile, he caresses me then takes off my pants. When we are sufficiently aroused and I have a jock strap, I straddle him, spreading my thighs wide. His cock tenderly sinks into my body then it's me who moves back and forth at my own pace. When he goes to cum, he takes my penis in hand to masturbate it, which makes us cum together. That's wonderful.

We also make love in the fitting room. In hypermarkets, we go to the cabin and there, I undo his fly to suck him. When he's hot enough,

I pull down my panties, place my hands on a wall, staying straight and spreading my legs wide so he can take me from behind. It excites us a lot to hear people talking around us and to cum during this time. When he feels his juices rising, he moves his hand in front of me to grab my little cock and masturbate it. We cum together most of the time. The problem is that his cum leaks out of my ass when we leave. The first time, I let myself be fooled. Now Max buys me some tampax and I shove one up my ass by the time I get home.

At home, I always mop the floor on all fours. I wear a large t-shirt and don't wear panties. No need to tell you what happens to me if Max is in the house. He first admires my thighs, then approaches to caress them. Then he fingers me to fully dilate me. When he feels that I have a good hard-on, he pushes his beautiful organ deep inside me.

All this to tell you all of my happiness in living with my man, whether it's to relieve him when his balls are full or to have some really enjoyable sex sessions.

My friend Maeva

I'm going to tell a story that I had with my girlfriend.

Her name is Maeva, she's 26 years old, light brown hair, even blond, very long, reaching the lower back. Light blue eyes, a fairly large natural chest, rounded buttocks worked by dancing which she has practiced since she was little.

She is 1m62 and weighs 52 kg.

We have been together for 9 years, we entered into a civil partnership when we were 5 years together.

In terms of sex, we feel like the first day, no worries on that side.

She works in a pantyhose store, she often wears them, I am a bit of a fetishist but I never admitted it to her, then, I dreamed of fucking her with her pantyhose.

Apart from that, to make ends meet, she sells pantyhose and other lingerie on the black market.

The story begins when she received a message from a new customer, who was interested in pantyhose and lingerie.

After work, she goes to this client's. She comes home late.

M. Baby, I need to talk to you!

I listen to her carefully.

M. The client I went to see offered to make videos for a pornographic site for money.

I really wasn't enthusiastic and I was seriously jealous.

M. Of course, it's not advanced stuff but we need this money if we want to move out of this apartment.

She wasn't wrong about that, we've been living in 20m2 for 3 years.

I ask her anyway, what is he asking you for, which site, etc.

M. I didn't accept it, I really wanted to talk to you about it first!

That reassures me, so I don't want her to do that.

M. We really need it. It's not with my salary or yours.

I let her explain.

M. It will be on this site, my head will be blurred and there will be no sex.

That reassures me a little but then why do it on a site..

The next day, she comes home a little late and tells me what she did with this guy.

I had to find out about this guy, she tells me he was dark-skinned, he's 48, tall and thin.

I thought to myself what kind of pervert is this.

She shows me on the site, her head is indeed very blurred, photos of her in tights and ultra sexy lingerie.

I giggle several times.

A week ago, she went to his place every evening. I went to see on the site what he was doing, more photos of my girlfriend with her face blurred.

One day, she comes home and comes straight to see me.

Mr. Baby, don't get angry please!

I was expecting something horrible.

Mr. I jerked off the customer with my feet.

I was upset.. She reassured me by telling me not to worry, she was mainly doing it for the money. I could only believe her, she has never done this to me in 9 years.

Curious and jealous as the plague, I went to the profile of this guy, "Mohammed".

There was indeed a video, I launched it and I saw the nightmare, my girlfriend lying on the edge of the bed, the man sitting opposite. My girlfriend's feet clad in pantyhose jerking off a huge cock.

I was shocked by the size of the cock, it is much longer than mine.

I move forward in the video, he held her feet to speed up the back and forth.

The man moaned.

H. It's so good, yeah!

He ejaculated on a tissue.

I thought he was going to cum on her feet.

I decided to talk about it because it really bothers me.

She told me not to worry that it was going to end.

The next day, she comes home instead.

I ask him, haven't you gone to see your client?

M. No, he offered me sodomy, I refused and left.

I was hallucinating...I didn't know if I should believe her anymore. I'm going back to this site with no video. It's okay, I'm reassured.

One Sunday afternoon, this man sent a message to my girlfriend to tell her to come by.

She accepts and tells me.

M. If he offers me something dirty I won't accept and I'll leave.

I searched his site to get more information on this guy but nothing appears. We see him, he is very old, then we see my girlfriend. A dialog was already installed.

H. I offer you this amount and you masturbate in front of me and I jerk off.

He's sick, I couldn't reach Maeva, his cell phone must have been on silent. M. No, it's dead, I'm not doing that.

H. By keeping your clothes!

M. Okay, I'll keep my clothes.

She was dressed in a black cotton mini skirt, with a white blouse. If you pay close attention, you can see a burgundy red lace bra.

She had on a pair of light black tights with reinforcements on the feet. Fine black lace panties.

She had put her hair in a simple bun.

I said to myself no, I'm living a nightmare.

I see her lie down on the edge of the bed, spread her thighs, then touch her pussy.

The man sat opposite, naked, jerking off.

H. You are so good!

He was wanking gently. Then his cock grew very quickly. I was stunned, she was big.

My girlfriend speeds up her movements from looking at the guy's big cock. I was wondering why she does that.

H. For that one more thing, will you let me stick my dick in?

M. Uuuh!

H. Just stick to nothing else!

Mr. Okay

But what is she doing seriously..

He gets up and sticks his cock on Maeva's pussy, obviously there are her tights and her panties.

I'm speechless, I can't believe it...

He rubs his cock above and grabs one of Maeva's feet to lick it. My girlfriend's face transformed, she had turned completely red.

M. We should stop there!

He stops licking his feet

H. I know you don't want to.

He lies on top of her and rubs his cock harder.

H. Let it happen.

He goes down on her pussy and rips off her pantyhose.

I was going crazy, I tried to call his phone, nothing helped, I didn't even know where he lived, then the live, my girlfriend isn't even blurry. She got tricked.

He gave her cunnilingus. I heard my girlfriend cum, I didn't even want to look at the screen anymore. It lasted for a while...

When I turned on the PC, after 10 minutes, she was naked, she had kept her tights on and her little panties out of place. His gaze lost, his head red as a tomato.

He takes her bareback missionary... back and forth that lasts and lasts.

I roll my eyes. I couldn't watch anymore.

But 15 minutes later, I went back to it.

She was on top of him, getting fucked, she was moaning, I was freaking out when I saw them kissing each other.

His big cock moving hugely in and out.

My inexperienced girlfriend doesn't move so much.

She only knew me as a sexual partner.

Then this guy.

I was really angry with myself and I should have even stopped people from going.

He takes her doggy style like a little submissive, he pulls her hair.

The most awful thing, I still said to myself, he fucked her with her stockings on, what a shame in 9 years of marriage..

Then, came the moment of ejaculation.

H. You have to suck me!

He didn't really give her a choice.

She was already on all fours, she opened her mouth, with small thrusts in her mouth, he ejaculated by placing both hands on the sides of Maeva's head, forcing her to swallow his sperm.

H. Yeah!

He approaches the camera and cuts it.

I'm living a nightmare.

I waited 2 hours before she came home.

The video was posted on his site.

My girlfriend came home and came to see me.

She made me a huge apology...

I didn't know if I should accept.

I ask him to never see this guy again.

My colleague Betty...

At the start of my career I worked in an office building, in an administration with fairly elderly women... I was very young at the age of 23, it was the second summer that I worked in these offices.

In the department that week there were 2 of us and the secretary... And there were a few people in the other departments including Betty (pseudo). A woman who was approaching forty, physically good, often dressed in a classy but very sexy manner...

The coffee machine and therefore the smoking room at the time was located close to her office, so I had to pass in front of her office to access it . And as she was alone she often followed me to chat and spend time with me over coffee, so we got to know each other better and she told me about her private life.

She was in a relationship but her boyfriend made fun of her according to her. She questioned me more and more about mine...

Moreover the summer before I had come across her by chance in a funfair in the south where I was with my friends. That day I was well written, she reminded me, telling me that I had been very relaxed with her unlike everyday life...

Still this week she offered to come and eat with me on the pretext that she had not brought anything unlike her usual, something which I did not refuse.

She had white pants that revealed her thong and a very beautiful neckline.

She asked me where I was going to eat, I told her McDonald's (classy, isn't it?), I offered her a drink first, it was hot and I wanted a cold beer, she told me OK. We sat down on the terrace, she drank a jet27 and after a while she told me that it was making her head spin (normal in full sun) and she would start to relax... We laughed wildly when she dropped a peanut on her neckline... (I really wanted to go get it myself) we then went to eat at Mc Do still laughing, we thought we were on vacation but very quickly I reminded him that we had to go to work a little , she said to me strangely

"Ah yes... but it's hot today, isn't it? » I replied to her "yes, very hot... we would be better off in the pool..." but I didn't think she would react by telling me "Chick???" » I turned completely red (fortunately with a matte complexion it's not visible).

I told her that I had no business and she suggested that I go get some towels at her place but since she had to buy a swimsuit we could end up at Decathlon and I would just have to buy a pair of swimming trunks... The appointment was made in front of Decathlon. I told the secretary something stupid and left!!!

I found her in front. We went back together to do our shopping, I took a pair of tight-fitting underwear and a very low-cut swimsuit (now I thought that was seriously provocative...)

Direction the swimming pool, we followed each other and when we arrived there, we settled down far from the crowd at her request. She put her towel down near mine. We bathe while holding each other close, more and more, then we lie down she asks me to put the cream on her back, something that I did wonderfully delicately on the neck then the hips, the back, then the top of the buttocks I felt her moan slightly then I go over the legs going up on her thigh, she moved her buttocks like an invitation to go up even higher, I felt her very excited, I did not dare to touch the buttocks ... Then she suddenly says to me "me!!!" I lay on my back. She massaged me very delicately but she dared the buttocks ...

She leaned over me, I felt her breasts on my back, I started to harden seriously, I was afraid to turn around in this state, especially with these tight underwear.

She insisted with her massage, I was in heaven... then I felt a kiss on my neck and a voice whispered to me "I want you, for you to make love to me....

A day that starts well

Saturday morning at 7am, I was thinking of sleeping in, but habit means I'm awake. I wrap my arms around my wife and lean against her back. I slide my hand under her pajama top and place it on her breast. I start to caress her breast and play with her nipple which I knead between my thumb and index finger.

Not a word, but she doesn't complain either. I gently move my hand down her stomach and under her pajama bottoms. I try to slide it between her thighs which she keeps tight, preventing me from caressing her pussy. I feel a well-shaped pubic area like a metro ticket that she had to make last night. I try to reach her clit and caress it with my finger, that's when she emerges and whispers in my ear, "Wouldn't we read a little story?" »

My darling loves reading HDS, those between women or for the first time » make her wet like a real slut She takes her phone and starts looking for the story that will please her and transform her into a real slut open to everything. When she is hot she just asks to be taken in every hole and to be fucked to the dregs. It is in this state that she will suck my glans, swallow it to the hilt and let herself caress the little hole, letting me insert one then two fingers there.

While she reads and gets excited, I take out the vibrator and sweet almond oil spray from the nightstand. I start to caress her with the tip of the vibrator and knead her nipples. She spreads her legs gently so that I can pass the vibrator all over her pussy which is getting wetter and harder.

I pull down her pajama bottoms and I continue to caress her gently, passing the vibrator between her lips until I place it on her tight little corolla. I press lightly and the tip sinks slightly into my darling's little hole. I go back to take care of her pussy and push the 25 cm of the machine into her dripping wet sex. I get hard like crazy watching the lips open and swallow the vibrator.

At the same time she strokes her clit with one hand while reading her story. I start to place my middle finger on her rosette and turn it to stick a finger in her ass. Quickly she swallows my first phalanx then my whole middle finger which moves back and forth in her ass which is lubricated more and more.

After a little while I take out my finger, leave the vibrator she is grabbing stuck in her pussy and I jerk off while watching her jerk off. Her pussy is glistening wet. "I want to cum, she tells me," "Calm down and take care of me and my cock." She takes out the vibrator and sucks it, while I lie down next to her. "So this story, she was "Yes, but now I'm horny as hell, and we're going to do the same thing as what I read" her kissing me. With my head between her legs, I part her lips with my fingers and slide my tongue into her pussy. I lapped at her clit hungrily. My chin is soaked with her juice. I slide a finger into his ass. She won't last long at this rate.

"Fuck me" she says to me while I am eating her clit, a finger stuck in her ass.

"Get on your knees" On my knees with my buttocks in the air, I stand behind her and grab both of her buttocks which I spread to see her pussy and her little hole. I slide two fingers into her soaked sex and I jerk her off eagerly.

I take my fingers out and place them on his little ring to lubricate it. I move forward to lick her puck but my darling has never liked this practice and gently pushes me away. So I walk past her and place my cock in her face. The message is very clear and well understood.

She runs her tongue over my glans and plays with it, while caressing my balls with her hand. She slides a finger between my buttocks and caresses my ring. I want to let go of everything, it's so good. She goes down the hard shaft and licks it along its entire length.

After a few minutes of this treatment I reposition myself behind her ass and slide my cock into her open pussy. I pound her ardently, holding her by the buttocks while slipping a thumb into her ass. She strokes her clit from underneath while I continue to fuck her pussy. "Put your cock instead of your finger," she whispers to me. "I pull out of her dripping wet sex and retrieve the vibrator which I turn on again.

"I'm going to take you from the front and from behind," I told him, sliding the device into her pussy, spreading his penis apart with the other hand. "Hold it in and jerk off while I fill your little hole." She grabs the vibrator and holds it in her crack. I grab the sweet almond oil spray and spray it on the puck. I massage her little ring with my thumb which I gently push into her dilated anus. I hear him breathing harder and harder with his head buried in the pillow. I stick my cock on his washer and press gently.

My glans easily fits into her ass, well lubricated by the oil. I continue to press and insert my entire rod. I fuck her while kneading her nipples. I feel the vibrator vibrating gently through her perineum. The feeling is sensational.

"Darling, I'm going to cum, oh that's good" I continue my thrusts in her ass and I feel my balls slapping against her pussy filled with the vibrator. "I'm going to let go of everything I tell her" I take my cock out of her ass and I jerk off on her buttocks while she continues to polish her pussy and I spray her with several well-filled jets.

Our enjoyment was strong and we lay down next to each other to recover.

A day that starts well...

Alone with my wife: she lets go

On vacation for a few days as a family, my wife and I find ourselves alone for 3 days. While I was preparing the appetizer, my wife, who was tapping on her phone, said to me in a sweet voice, "darling, I want you".

I turn around to serve her cup and I see her on the sofa with her legs crossed in the lotus position, her dress pulled up and her hand in her panties. She was caressing her pussy. I put down her cup and move towards her to kiss her.

I slip my tongue into his mouth and slide my hand between his legs to join his. "Slip me a finger and jerk me off." I pull down her panties to have easy access to her already wet sex and I stick my middle finger in and start moving back and forth rather slowly to begin with.

A splashing sound accompanies the movements of my finger. I get my darling up to unfold the sofa into a bed, she lies down on it, legs spread, her gaping pussy open to all possible penetrations.

I position myself in front of her, on my knees and start fingering her again. "Guess how many I'll slip you" "Two" she said to me. With a big smile I continue to finger her with my index and middle fingers. She is soaked, the sheet is stained so much that her pussy is leaking. I slide a third finger into her open sex and got wet as ever. " And now ".

While she is having fun with her eyes closed while caressing her breasts, my darling whispers "three, keep jerking me off, it's so good".

On my knees between her open thighs I masturbate her with one hand and I jerk off with the other. I am fascinated by this spectacle of her pussy penetrated by my fingers. I take pleasure in taking them completely out and in, spreading her lips with my other hand. I also love taking my cock and patting her soaking wet sex. "You like watching me caress myself or insert a finger into me," she said to me.

"I love it, it excites me terribly, take my cock in your hand, you will understand the effect it has on me" She encloses my rod between her fingers and begins to jerk me off, while I continue to finger her "I brought the vibrators, they are in the suitcase, take them" I regretfully leave the inside of her wet pussy to go get our two vibrators.

Back in the living room of our apartment, I see my darling lighting a cigarette. She loves it when we smoke while fucking. She draws on her cigarette then blows the smoke towards me with a slutty look. She goes down to her pussy and caresses her pussy while holding her cigarette. I turn on the vibrator and pass it over her penis, spreading her labia apart.

After a few minutes, I straighten the vibrator and push it into her pussy. She swallows it completely. I have fun taking it in and out while changing gears. My darling is in heaven. I give her the vibrator so she can continue masturbating. She pushes it into her pussy, takes it out and caresses her clit, passing it over her erect nipples.

Meanwhile, I caress her little hole. I turn my finger over it and push it in gently.

Once my middle finger is firmly planted in her ass I begin to move quickly back and forth which makes her moan. While continuing to finger her ass, I lie down between her legs and start licking her button, while she still has the vibrator buried deep in her pussy.

I hear him moan and whisper "oh that's good" "keep going, fuck me" "fuck my ass". I stop for a moment to borrow her cigarette, I blow the smoke on her sex and I resume lapping her pussy.

"I'm going to cum," she told me while arching her back. I stop my cunnilingus and take my finger out of her ass so as not to make her cum.

"Take care of me," I tell her. I lie down next to her, she takes the vibrator out of her little wet cave and places herself on her knees, her head next to my cock. She starts to run her tongue over the tip of my cock while caressing my balls.

After a little while of treatment she swallows my rod entirely and sucks me like never before. I feel a finger pass over my washer and gently dig in. I'm so happy. She pivots and places her pussy above my head. We launch into a magnificent 69. I take the opportunity to take care of his eyelet.

I can't wait, I turn her on her back, lift her legs and sink into her dripping pussy. My balls slap against her ass. She pinches her nipples and encourages me to fuck her harder.

"Take me by the ass," she said to me. I slipped a cushion under her eyelash and placed my cock on her washer. Softened by my fingers previously, my penis enters without problem. I sodomize her deeply while she caresses her pussy.

At the end of a moment, my darling retrieves the vibrator and places it in her sex She is taken by her two orifices. The orgasm arrives and we cum simultaneously, I only have time to take out my cock for me and my sperm squirt on her .

She gets it from there and licks her fingers languorously. She takes out the vibrator and sucks it to recover the salty juice from her little pussy. We lie down while kissing for a long time.

The afternoon and this weekend without children starts well.

Rebuilding your relationship

I discovered a month ago that my wife had been cheating on me on and off for three years with one of her friends. I had access to the exchanges she had on her email. Among other things, she wrote him stories about their relationship. That's how I learned that she was sucking him and that he had licked her pussy. I even found out that he came in her mouth and she swallowed, even though she doesn't like it.

She assured me that this relationship was an escape from our life which had become non-existent and even harmful. We haven't had any contact for several months.

We decided to resolve our relationship problem. We still love each other and we wanted to rebuild ourselves.

One morning when I was up and after discussing this relationship my wife called me. I joined her in the room with some fruit juice. My darling was lying on the bed, her nightie pulled up. She was caressing her pussy. She looked me in the eyes and said "I want to fuck darling, take the cigarettes and the toys". Time to take the cigarettes and her vibrators, I find her naked slipping a finger into her pussy and caressing her breasts with the other hand.

"Give me the cigarettes and pet me." » While she lights her cigarette I turn on the vibrator and start to tickle her clit. I caress her pussy with it and start to penetrate her. Her wet sex swallows the vibrator with ease. I move back and forth, taking the vibrator out completely.

"Keep going, it's so good," she said to me while caressing her penis.

I continue to fuck her with the vibrator and I lie down between her thighs to kiss her and lick her clit. My darling takes the vibrator from me to fuck her pussy, she pinches her nipples with her other hand while I continue to lap at her little asshole. I begin to caress her little hole by gently rotating with my finger that I had previously wet by sliding it into her pussy along the vibrator. I first inserted one knuckle, then two and finally my entire middle finger. I felt the toy vibrate in his little back door.

"Go ahead and fuck me in the ass, give me a second one," she said, looking into my eyes. I slipped a second finger into her which went in easily as she was so relaxed.

"Do you like it" I asked him

"It's so good to be fucked in the ass with the vibrator in your pussy".

After a good while of this little game I lay down next to her. I caress her breasts and suck her nipples. I think it's time for you to take care of me, I tell him, stroking my tail. She removed the vibrator from her penis and placed herself between my legs. She took my penis in her hands and started to jerk me off. She delicately runs her tongue over my glans and along my shaft. Suddenly she swallowed my cock and sucked me with a sucking noise. She let some saliva flow so she could jerk me off at the same time.

"it's okay, keep going", "lick my balls".

She tried to run her tongue over my balls and take them in her mouth while polishing my cock. I wanted to release everything in her mouth and flood her throat but I wanted even more to slide into her sex and sodomize her. She turned on me to present her pussy to me. I lapped his cock with big licks, which went up to his little hole. Discreetly I licked her corolla.

"Go get my ass ready," she whispered to me.

After having moistened her ass well and slipped a finger back into her, I got behind her with my penis in hand. I rubbed it against her open and wet slit and with one thrust I penetrated her. She was panting, getting wetter and wetter under the harder and harder thrusts I was giving her. She passed her hand between her legs to caress herself violently. She stretched out her arm to come and caress my balls which hung under her sex.

They were hard and full to the brim. My wife must have sensed it because it was at that moment that she said to me: "you want to put it in my ass".

She lies on her back and slides a pillow under her buttocks. I take the opportunity to advance my penis in front of her mouth. She runs her tongue over the glans and swallows my cock along its entire length. I feel her tongue swirl around my cock. She sucks my rod while I hold her head with my hand. I ended up withdrawing so as not to cum in his mouth.

I grab the vibrator that was still working and push it into her pussy. My wife came and felt the dildo vibrate deep inside her.

"Hold it and get high with it."

I bring my cock closer to his little puck and start to press. My glans enters her conduit without difficulty. I fuck her in the ass while taking my cock out and in several times. Taken twice by the vibrator and my penis, she was on the verge of pleasure.

"I'm going to cum," she said. I take my cock out of his little ring and jerk off in front of his face, which I spray with long, creamy jets. She wiped her face with her fingers and licked them clean.

We lay down to recover. My darling fell back asleep in my arms.

Fucked like a whore in a rebeu city

How I was subjugated by my father's best friend.

My father's best friend is quite a handsome man, Italian, in his thirties, tall, dark-haired...

I've often fantasized about him and his brother-in-law's cock, it looks XXL through his shorts... yum.

One day he asked me if I would like to go on vacation for a month with him and his brother-in-law. They had rented a small house in Italy on the coast.

Jumping at the opportunity to be on vacation with these two beautiful appolons, I accepted with great pleasure.

So we left by car two weeks later, I am a tall young man, just 18 years old, I have eyes that change color depending on the weather, black hair with lips that would make any girl melt, but too bad for them I'm 100% gay!!!

In the car, I slept for a long time because we had left really early. The brother-in-law of my father's friend, let's call them David, and Mauro was staring at me during my sleep, I know because I woke up... He was telling Mauro that I was too horny...

When we got home, after Having taken a tour of the house I noticed that there was only one bed in the house and that in a small windowless room there was a cage. I jokingly told them that I would take the cage, but they told me that it would be my room for the stay. I didn't notice that David was tearing off my clothes, telling me that I wouldn't need to wear them; instead of my boxers, he pulled up a little black leather thong tightly in my little line.

He was extremely surprised that I had gotten hard, and he told Mauro that I was a good cock-hungry whore and that they were going to have a lot of fun during that month.

Mauro called us for supper, but there were only two place settings, with a vicious smile he told me to go under the table if I wanted to eat.

Resigning me, he undid the buttons of his jeans to push a 25 x 5 cm stake into me. Needless to say, I almost suffocated. After an hour of a very wet blowjob, he grabbed me by the hair and squirted 5-6 salty jets deep into my tonsils.

Then the bell rang and the door opened to reveal 5 super handsome young people who said they had rented me for the night. I saw wads of notes leave Maomed's pocket and end up in Mauro's hands. During the car ride they stuck a size 4 plug in me and told me that their new slave was going to be fucked by their entire city and forced me to suck a young rebel who released his juice deep inside me.

In the city I had to get on my knees while they cum in my mouth. Then one of them forced me to drink his urine and told me that if a drop got on my sucking lips, my ass would not recover...

After having drunk it all and almost vomited another one dried his cock on me in the foundation and plowed me for 30 minutes, he was enduring the bastard, after his ejaculation, about 50 rebeus of the city stuck their cocks into me and at the end they slid like butter.

Back at home I got fucked by David who is about 30cm by 8cm. Damn he had to force it and I was crying when he told me to swallow his cum...

Maria across the street

Maria is my next door neighbor, I live in a building of around twenty people. I know a few of them but nothing more except Maria whom I meet at least every other day and who talks constantly...

I manage to tiptoe out of my house, because if she accosts me, it is screwed. She spends half an hour talking to you about everything and nothing and honestly it's not very interesting.

One winter morning, my car no longer wanted to start...at -2°.

No doubt hearing my numerous starts, she came to see what was wrong, she is also very curious. I explain to him that the car won't start and that I will have to go to work by taxi.

She insisted that I take her car, "I don't need it today" she told me, "take it, it doesn't bother me at all". So I accepted, which suited me too, I must admit.

A little aside regarding Maria, she must be around 45/50 years old, she lives alone, I think she has a daughter, who comes to see her from time to time. She has lived in the building for several years because I have always known her. She is well preserved for her age, she is goodness itself, she is always there to help but what is she talking!

I think the whole building is avoiding her because of that...I notice that it's always my house that she comes to, for a yes or a no, no eggs, no more salt, she was looking for my mail , she offers me a bottle of digestive from her country, she lends me her car, she cleans my room, receives my registered mail and parcels...

Either she really likes me, or she has no one else to talk to.

That day, when I brought her car back to her and wanted to thank her, I offered, with a little reluctance, to come and eat at my place on Saturday evening, as a thank you. An invitation that she accepted without hesitation.

Good or bad thing...we'll see on Saturday.

Saturday 6:30 p.m., there is a knock on the door, I open it and there is Maria with her arms full of packages. I bring her in and the chatter begins, "I brought, here is pâté and cheese from Poland for you (she was born in Kielce), my brother also makes alcohol himself, very strong but good smelling".

And here I am with lots of products that are certainly excellent, but it's going to take a year to eat them all...

While I take care of all this, make yourself comfortable, take off your coat, I'm coming.

I put everything in the kitchen and when returning to the living room, I saw her without her long coat... red skirt, black stockings and cream blouse, she is all made up and perfumed. I have a little trouble recognizing our Maria, apart from her whore look, she remains a beautiful woman.

We sit in the living room opposite, and the aperitif begins. She tells me about the building, her family, her cat who ran away, her daughter who doesn't come to see her very often , from his hometown....

2 hours without being able to place one..., by the way, she no longer wants Mrs. K.............,

But Maria does.

We sit down at the table and then the tone changes, she asks me questions and curiously...she listens to me without interrupting me, which is quite unusual. She seems interested in my job and my family, come on! It's nice...she's not such a pain in the ass after all.

During the meal, I keep staring at her red bra which appears under her blouse, it's really in bad taste, but it has an effect on me.

The meal continues in an excellent atmosphere, and the wine goes down very quickly...the second bottle is almost dead! Well, she has a good descent Maria, that gives her color, also to me.

The third bottle is heavily started, the discussion turns and becomes more intimate, she talks to me about loneliness since her divorce (alcoholic husband), she no longer has any friends here because they returned to the country, she has the impression that the other tenants avoid her because she always causes (That's not wrong).

Men are no longer interested in her, I try to comfort her in clothes, let's not forget that she could almost be my mother...

She tells me that at 48, she still knows how to deal with men, and that anyone who would like to take a little interest in her would not regret it.

Excited as a goat, I banged the boner of the year, titanium!

I had to get up to serve dessert, but with a boner like that, tough (that's fair to say)

After a few minutes she gets up to go to the bathroom, I take the opportunity to clean up and watch her too...I need to calm down!

Back from the waters, she sits down again and says to me "if you want to taste my brother's alcohol, it is very good for digestion". Come on, let's try...

I serve everyone a small glass, which must be drunk in one go. And suddenly... Ugh, this stuff is Kerosene, it's goat's hoof juice or something... it decreases in any case.

"If you want we can move on to dessert, if you still have a little room" I told him.

"I have two or three desserts to offer you, it depends on your tastes"

"I eat everything, chosen for us, don't take everything out of the fridge"

.....................small blank (of reflections)

Well if it's I choose the dessert, I choose you!

(Today, several months after that evening, I still don't know why I told him that...a real stupid thing)

I saw her turn red, me too, not really knowing how to react, I took her hand and told her that I really like her (with the help of alcohol) and that I really want her (it's very hollow, but hey...).

I get up, she too, we look into each other's eyes and I kiss her, slipping my hands under her blouse. She sticks her tongue in my mouth, unbuttons my jeans gently.

Hands slide over her buttocks and it's still very firm!

I find myself with the jeans on my ankles and my boxers follow very quickly, she kneels and begins to suck me thoroughly, I resisted for less than a minute!! She swallowed everything without stopping...hoolala the night is going to be long...

Maria takes off my jeans and boxers and takes me by the hand towards the bedroom, I just ejaculate like an ox and my boner continues...She asks me to lie down on the bed and sit astride my stomach. Maria takes off her blouse which is flying in the corner of the room and then comes to her support. Not a bad chest, it hangs a little but there is substance. She kisses me while unbuttoning my shirt, she kisses my chest, my nipples, my navel and again a shorter blowjob this time. My penis is fully erect, she holds it with one hand and licks my balls.

So good, I'm going crazy I'm going to die!!!

Then she positions herself on top of me again and impales herself on my cock, in fact she is not wearing any panties!!! And presto, the back and forth begins and I give, I give.....and I unload...wow she knows how to move in any case. She pulls out and washes me!!!

We are now lying side by side on my bed, she still has her skirt and stockings on.

I caressed her for a long time. "How about we take a bath now?" » she said to me, okay for the bath. I turn on the hot water, a few scoops of essential oils and some candles for ambiance. Maria enters the bathroom completely naked with a slight smile, (she is really well built for her age) she walks towards me and kisses me greedily.

We took a bath together, she soaped me and me too and we returned to the room for the second round, I took care of her. It was really great, I think we fell asleep around 4am.

We have been together for 8 months, Maria was right, she knows how to take care of men. About 14 years separate us and yet I am very in love with him, we almost live together because we see each other so often. Living on the same level creates bonds.

Moment between dream and eternity

Repeat after me and enter my universe: Jisom Tuex Ico...Jisom Tuex Ico...Jisom Tuex Ico...Now you are ready to read me...

You are the comet that penetrated my solar system, my balance and caused me to lose my orbit . Your blue eyes met me as I left this banal underground parking lot, a reflection of the disinterest I feel for this world.

From cold reality, to the warmest dream of you. Beautiful child of Venus in this pretty tight-fitting jumpsuit, rebellious biker, disruptive spawn of the Universe. Your curves are a sin that I would like to taste. I give you a look that contains all my desire and my desire, both unspeakable. You meet him; You know. Unknown, but already on an immediate and common wavelength.

My mind and thoughts on the silver platter that is my soul. No need to speak, we speak the same language, incomprehensible to those who express it with words and not their Being. You smile at me with the look that says yes, I take your hand and pull you towards me.

Show me your beautiful white teeth as you laugh, beautiful stars in your eyes, pulsing. Am I desperate not to have you in my arms even though I don't know you?

You respond to me by drawing my hand to your soft and fine face, but it is your lips that respond to me when you insert my finger between them...

Your passionate tongue surrounds my body with unfathomable thrills in the depths of the inexpressible...

I am disarmed by your charms, your gaze freezes me and burns me, incandescent.

Endless waiting on the staircase of our desire...how far away our palace of delights is. At the top of the tower of desire, behind heavy doors that fall one after the other with each kiss and each passionate stop. I corner you in a corner, thinking I'll surprise you, but each time you welcome me into the den of your leather-encircled thighs, as if you read me like an open book.

Each of your looks undresses me a little more, my being reveals itself despite itself. No mask, even if only a broad smile on your lips, which you hasten to bite. Let me caress you and enclose your voluptuous forms between my fingers full of desire.

I would have liked to model you like my most unspeakable fantasies, but you are already the unexpected queen, surpassing them by far, at your knees you trample them with your perfection...

Malicious monarch, empress of my desire when you breathe my ear your wildest desires, farandole of fantasies, dance with me...

Would I have believed that it was you who pushed the door to my room to draw me into your dreamlike web, beautiful creature with ruddy eyes? Superhuman, like my desire, when you hold it in your breasts. Magnified Spawn of Chaos, you begin at the end before rushing back to the beginning. Let me take your zipper down from the bottom to the top, since nothing is true, everything is permitted. The complexion of your skin, white as innocence, pays a heretical homage to your damned passion.

Before kissing your thigh, here I am finding perdition in the crook of your neck, while marrying the curvature of my back with your wet delight... Is it not my neck that you are biting? I never thought I would tremble so much... The mountains of your wonders, reasonable Everests, slide into my mouth, I head you in search of your Substance... your true principle which would allow me the simple supposition of what you are, while you make me shiver by holding me in your arms...

I surrender to your gaze, when I discover you in your simplest form. Is it the spot on your neck that reminds me of an 8-pointed star?

Your only response is a groan when I explore the entrance to your secret Universe with a greedy mouth in search of a new flavor. Your glistening pleasure flowing down my chin: bless me, beautiful Goddess, for I sin by feeling your hips tense like my penis ready to spring!

Is it discovered by your dripping intimacy, or the tropical sweetness of your throat?

Let me grab hold of your hair, hold it tight as if to prevent me from falling backwards... Where can it be you that I accompany in the fall and the ecstasy?

Your thighs respond to me and hug me. Could I have ever imagined that entering into the creation of the world would be so ecstatic? It is no longer my body that you envelop, it is passion itself, ardent and hard like my mortal existence. What are you looking for in my eyes, while I pierce you with my body, so you take away all reason from me? Your irises dilate and I can feel it too in the hollow of your hips.

Let me race on horseback around all the planets in the galaxy...your butt is such a beautiful illustration. You may be offered to me in body, but in truth, you hold my pleasure on a leash, gripped by your little lips which could whisper: "Take me". Your mind is my prison, my pleasure, your temple. And by rushing at me with each movement, sudden and intense, you prove me wrong.

Have I fallen unconscious while you kiss my lips? Here you are in front of me, a big smile on your lips, insolent. Would I completely lose control, subjected to the delicious undulations of your pelvis? There seems to be no limit to the depth of your body and your mind. And the more our bodies merge, the more magical the moment is. Do you also feel the shivers that assail my body? Each glance at your revealed chest ecstasies me a little more.

From life to death, feeling of absolute pleasure, you kiss me to offer me absolution. Your sudden interruption to make me rediscover the lair of your most exciting words is a delight that looks more like a gourmet dessert than an appetizing appetizer... I hold myself back from exploding and you enjoy it by delighting in this frustration without closing your mouth...

Come back to me, beautiful Amazon, capture my soul by impaling yourself again on the manifestation of my pleasure and take a malicious pleasure in arching your back languorously. Tie me to the rise of your pleasure like a volcano in sensory eruption.

Yes, that's it, close your eyes. You enter a trance, dragging me into your madness.

Let me delight in our pleasures on the edge of total fulfillment. Your cry is a deliverance, the torture of containing my orgasmic urge is as harsh as the few pelvic thrusts that I dare to give you so that your enjoyment is total. Your bluish and fulfilled gaze comes to beg, accompanied by a nibbling of the lip, that I abandon myself in you to delicious waves of burning and humid pleasure...

How to resist you, when you come to shiver against my body, bringing me the warmth of your breasts and a sweet word. Each pulsation is a delicious gift to the depths of your intimacy... Is it your belly and the warmth of your skin that I feel when the last wave comes? When you seem to delight in rubbing your skin dripping with my happiness between our united bodies? You are the perfect incarnate...

Abandon yourself in my arms. I welcome you willingly and hold you against me. Let me whisper in your ear that my life will never be the same after having known such delight. Give me the pleasure of your smile in my ear, of a sigh of ease, of an unequaled tenderness, captivated by our lovemaking, outside of space and time, for a night or an eternity...

Let's start again...

The forest of pleasures

The weather was foggy that morning. Solène had visited her grandparents, in the middle of the Vercors. Their little house was far from everything, close to a large forest. In order to return home to Lyon, the young woman decided to take a regional bus, served once a day at a small bus stop in front of the big woods.

Placing her bag on the ground in front of her, she placed her butt on the cold bench of the bus shelter, staring at the road from side to side in search of a way to quickly return home. But nothing, not a car, nor the famous bus came after an hour of waiting.

Tired and wrapped up in her coat, she had a hard time not falling asleep. But the magic of the place gave way to daydreaming, then daydreaming. A fine drizzle covered this forest landscape, enhanced by a beautiful mist delicately hiding in the undergrowth.

If the weather was gray this autumn day, the atmosphere was deliciously fantastic.

Solène closed her eyes, allowing herself to take a carefree nap, resting her head against the wooden edge of the small improvised cocoon. A small, innocuous nap, which was nevertheless gently cut short by the strange sensation of being observed.

Solène revealed her gray gaze, searching for the source of a gaze that was passing over her. Then, she saw at the edge of the wood, a young man, who was looking at her, half hidden behind a tree. She sat up a little on her bench, not out of fear but caution.

The man then advanced towards her, crossing the road which separated them. It was then that the young girl noticed that this stranger was walking barefoot. His gait was light, slow, fluid and elegant. About 20 years old, the boy wore simple canvas clothes, visibly handmade, giving off a strange, wild and mysterious look. His face was thin, unshaven but without vulgarity, his slightly curly brown hair gave an impression of softness.

But what disturbed Solène the most were her eyes. Beautiful, large blue eyes, whose pupils were like spirals, small oceanic swirls, which seemed to rotate on themselves, giving an almost magical aura.

And it was the depth of this mysterious being's gaze that made her startle a little, standing up at his approach.

Don't worry, Solène, I mean you no harm. said the man, in a soft and suave voice, that of a dreaming young boy.

Who are you ? And...how do you know my name? she asked, almost offended at not being anonymous.

My name is Illias. And I've been waiting for you for a very long time. He replied, in a velvet voice devoid of any aggression.

You...you were waiting for me? she stammered, disturbed as much by the dialogue as by the beauty of this character.

I have been able to see your dreams, I have been watching over you for many years, waiting for you to come to meet me today.

Solène didn't know what to answer and couldn't move when he walked towards her to hold her hand.

Come with me, let's experience this moment outside of the passing of time...

And as he caressed her fingers, she felt herself moving towards the forest, accompanied by this man. Normally, she would probably be struggling, refusing to be taken into the unknown.

But something invaded his mind, like a soft dreamlike veil, spreading throughout his body a great impression of gentleness, love and trust. So she walked with him, not looking behind her so as not to see the road disappear, swallowed up by the forest.

And while the path seemed to last an eternity, hand in hand, they arrived in front of a splendid large tree, gigantic in fact, with a gnarled trunk, surrounded by a small clearing. Magic emanated from this place, which seemed not to be real. The cold drizzle had stopped moistening Solène's skin as she stroked the bark of this strange oak.

The man smiled when he saw her do this, then passing very close to her neck he blew a little hot air which made her shiver. He in turn touched the tree with his fingertips, which seemed to react and a large door appeared before their eyes.

Solène let herself be totally carried away by the magic of the moment, intoxicated by the charm of the place and of this man whom she found more and more handsome the more she looked at him...her heart palpitating in her chest.

They both entered a large recess in the trunk of the tree. The place was warm and welcoming. A small fire was burning in a corner, not far from large mats of dry leaves and feathers.

The door closed noiselessly, at the same time as the stranger's arms around Solène's shoulders, who shuddered at this contact. The light became more subdued. He traveled down the young woman's neck with a long breath full of desire and love. She couldn't contain a small breath of joy, seized by a great shiver that went down her spine.

The young woman's half-closed eyes were lost in the spirals of the pupils of this man who was offering her more pleasure than ever. But despite the erotic contact of her body against his, she gradually regretted not being free to offer him much more, at the limits of her body and her intimacy.

So she tried as best she could to lay him on his back. The latter allowed himself to be done, with a hint of amusement expressed by a slight bite on the neck.

Trembling with pleasure, she impaled herself lovingly on this hot penis, dripping with her excitement. Feeling him so deep inside her made her cum again. She activated her pelvis in large waves that seemed to twist Illias with pleasure, who no longer knew where to put his hands.

For a few minutes, it was the perfect union of pleasure and contained masculine excitement, in a beautiful duo of cries and moans.

And came the common orgasm, powerful, unpredictable and unconcerted, Solène who screamed louder, feeling her body stiffen with pleasure making her pleasure pulse in each of her veins. Her vagina contracted a little more at this discharge of pleasure, which came from the little willpower that remained in her lover, who began to cum, shouting in turn, deeply introduced into her.

She appreciated in this magical moment, as much her pleasure as the sensation of heat which invaded her in waves of pleasure, his burning semen which slipped inside her with so much love and passion...

And it was only after long minutes of nirvana that she let herself fall on him, exhausted, but fulfilled, feeling his warm arms hold her against him.

And then, his smile widened, before calming down...

Afternoon in the sauna

First of all I would like to make you understand who I am. For many years I felt deeply heterosexual, only having sex with women, and totally disgusted by all these homos (how stupid one can be), and then one day I admitted my bisexuality. It was by watching porn videos that I understood what excited me the most in these videos was fellatio.

In fact what I like about fellatio is watching the member when it comes out and goes into the girl's mouth, and yes women's bodies make me hard, but I feel great pleasure in looking at men's sexes, and only their sexes, I find no beauty even in the bodies of male athletes, strange no...

So one day I decided to test myself, I signed up on a dating site, and I took the plunge.

A few meetings with men, with the sole aim of practicing fellatio, all the meetings were not extraordinary but I have some good memories of them.

Then curiosity pushed me to the point of trying sodomy once, and ... I enjoyed it. Meetings via the internet are complex to organize and often end in fake dates. So I decided to try the libertine sauna.

Thanks to a friend who knows nothing about my bisexuality, I free myself from my wife one Saturday afternoon. My wife thinks we are going to the races and I let my friend believe that I have a mistress. Here I am finally in this place of pleasure, I am overwhelmed because at first glance I only see men, that's what I'm looking for.

After a quick tour I sat in a living room where an x-video is playing, two men are sitting and staring at the screen, they don't even turn their heads when I sit down near them.

One of the guys caresses himself under his towel, the other just watches the video. I start to caress myself under my towel, and as soon as I'm ready I open it to show my anatomy.

And then the guy who masturbates takes a quick look then returns to his film, I'm disappointed, probably straight straight guys. I leave the living room and go to the sauna, where I am alone, but I notice that the guys regularly stop by to look, I lie down on my towel and I start to caress myself.

In less than two minutes a guy comes in and sits next to me in the same position as me, I'll call him Pierre, he caresses himself while looking at me, which excites me even more. I offer to caress him to help him be more toned, he accepts but after a few seconds his cock is very hard and he asks me to suck it. I suggest we go to a private room, explaining to him that I would like to be taken, he is very excited and we leave the sauna.

In our small living room after putting a condom on him I start to suck him, it lasts several minutes, I like to suck and he seems to enjoy it, so I suggest he move on to the second stage when I notice behind me a guy who has entered without saying anything and who masturbates while watching us, it will be Alain, his penis tempts me, I suggest he come join me and ask him to put on a condom. Pierre caresses my anus with his fingers, I ask him to put some gel on, after a good preparation and while I suck Alain, Pierre introduces himself, I pump even harder on Alain's penis.

While I am caught between these two cocks, a third thief enters, he faces me, masturbates and as soon as his penis is bandaged he hands it to me, I remove Alain's penis from my mouth and ask It's up to Didier to put on a condom, he doesn't seem happy but he puts it on, so he puts his penis in my mouth, it's much bigger than that of my other two partners.

Pierre is still moving back and forth behind my back, but suddenly Didier grabs my head with both hands and pushes his cock into my throat several times quickly then he remains in pressure at the bottom, I believe for a moment that I'm going to turn away, but he withdraws in time, giving me just two seconds to regain my composure and starting the same session again, it's becoming a bit too hard for me, I pull away. I hadn't even noticed that Pierre had left his place to Alain, the latter was replaced by Didier who when he introduced himself did not leave me indifferent, the caliber was much bigger and I felt the difference, it's painful... I alternately suck Pierre and Alain while Didier massacres my anus, finally he withdraws, goes in front, takes off his condom and shoves his cock in my mouth. I don't even want to refuse, this guy is dominant I think I submit. Didier is suddenly gentler with me, I alternate between his cock and Pierre's and Alain takes me.

Suddenly Pierre, who no longer has a condom either, groans, I release his cock and masturbate him in front of my face, he then sends several beautiful squirts on my face, as soon as he is finished I I hear Alain let out a cry, he has just cum in my anus but he still has his condom on, Didier puts his cock back in my mouth but just as I feel that he is going to cum, he grabs my head to force me to take his sperm in my mouth, I give in and take a first squirt deep in my throat then he withdraws, I keep my mouth open and he finishes spraying me everywhere, I end up cleaning his cock with my tongue. The three guys left me with just a thank you, it was good.

I leave the small living room without wiping my face and chest which are covered in cum, I pass a few guys in the corridors and I head towards the showers. I face the shower and wash my face then my chest, my anus is on fire I offer him a wash which does not seem to soothe him, when I turn around two guys are standing in front of me and he is masturbating, the older asks me if I want some more, so I approach them and start sucking them without further delay, they come quite quickly and ejaculate almost at the same time on my face, this time I don't swallow not the sperm.

My afternoon is over, I am very happy with this experience, even if it remains painful for a few more hours. I hope it excited you as much as I did. I would definitely go back to the sauna, but next time I would stay more behaved. I am now waiting to meet a bi man and a woman for a very hot threesome.

To everyone who took the time to provide feedback, post reviews, or recommend our work to friends and loved ones – you have our undying appreciation. Knowing that our efforts resonate with so many individuals motivates us to continue pushing boundaries and breaking down barriers in pursuit of artistic excellence.

We hope that this second volume has provided ample opportunities for introspection, excitement, and escapism alike, further solidifying your trust in our ability to deliver top-quality content that speaks directly to your innermost desires. Rest assured that we remain committed to cultivating an ever-evolving library of exceptional literature aimed at enlightening minds and stirring loins across generations.

Should you feel compelled to share your own reactions, insights, or questions regarding "Twisted Intimacies Volume 2," please don't hesitate to reach out via social media, email, or direct message. Hearing from our readership helps shape future projects and fosters a sense of community built upon mutual respect, understanding, and open-mindedness.

Until next time, may your hearts beat faster, your skin tingle with anticipation, and your dreams be filled with the sweet fruits of twisted intimacies waiting just around the corner. Stay curious, fearless, and forever hungry for more!

Warm Regards,
Saicka Ross

Don't miss out!

Visit the website below and you can sign up to receive emails whenever Saicka Ross publishes a new book. There's no charge and no obligation.

https://books2read.com/r/B-A-FPTQB-QRSOD

BOOKS 2 READ

Connecting independent readers to independent writers.

Did you love *Twisted Intimacies*? Then you should read *Twisted Intimacies*[1] by Saicka Ross!

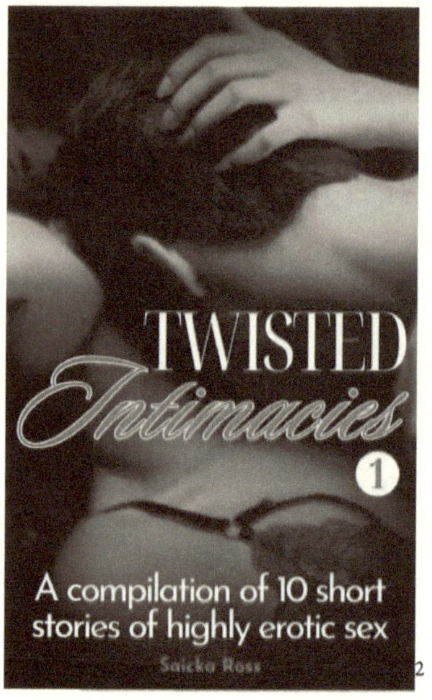

Immerse yourself in the world of passion and pleasure with my 1st collection of short sex stories, "Twisted Intimacies volume 1: A compilation of 10 short stories of highly erotic sex."

This enticing anthology brings together ten steamy shorts that will leave you breathless and craving more. From personal awakenings to chance encounters, each tale explores the depths of human desire in intimate detail.

With its diverse range of characters, settings, and situations, this collection offers something for everyone looking to explore the boundaries of sensuality and desire. So why wait? Dive into the pages of "Twisted Intimacies volume 1" today and let your imagination run wild!

---

1. https://books2read.com/u/bWyDLY

2. https://books2read.com/u/bWyDLY

Also by Saicka Ross

Twisted Intimacies
Twisted Intimacies
Twisted Intimacies